To Dad
On His Birthday
June 8/78
Your loving daughter
Brenda

McClelland and Stewart

FARLEY MOWAT

This Rock Within the Sea: A Heritage Lost

Photography by John de Visser

BOOKS BY FARLEY MOWAT

People of the Deer (1952, revised edition 1975)

The Regiment (1955, new edition 1973)

Lost in the Barrens (1956)

The Dog Who Wouldn't Be (1957)

Grey Seas Under (1959)

The Desperate People (1959, revised edition 1975)

Owls in the Family (1961)

The Serpent's Coil (1961)

The Black Joke (1962)

Never Cry Wolf (1963, new edition 1973)

Westviking (1965)

The Curse of the Viking Grave (1966)

Canada North (1967, revised paperback edition 1976)

This Rock Within the Sea (with John de Visser)
  (1968, reissued 1976)

The Boat Who Wouldn't Float (1969, illustrated edition 1974)

Sibir (1970, new edition 1973)

A Whale for the Killing (1972)

Wake of the Great Sealers (with David Blackwood) (1973)

The Snow Walker (1975)

Edited by Farley Mowat

Coppermine Journey (1958)

The Top of the World Trilogy

Ordeal by Ice (1960, revised edition 1973)

The Polar Passion (1967, revised edition 1973)

Tundra (1973)

First published 1968 by
Little, Brown and Company
in association with
the Atlantic Monthly Press, Boston
Reissued 1976 by
McClelland and Stewart Limited

ISBN: 0-7710-6632-5

The Canadian Publishers
McClelland and Stewart Limited
Illustrated Book Division
25 Hollinger Road, Toronto

Printed and bound in Canada

Design by Frank Newfeld

*We give this book
to the outport people
of Newfoundland.
We particularly give it
to the people of
Messieurs Cove,
and to Dorothy and
Doris Spencer who sang
songs in the days
of their childhood.*

When John de Visser and I resolved on the making of this book, we had in mind a mutual endeavour in which one art would complement the other in tenderly portraying the lineaments of a world we loved. This book was to have been our celebration of the closed universe of sea and rock, plants and beasts, wind and fog that occupies the primordial coasts of southern Newfoundland. But we particularly wished to celebrate the qualities of the people of that coast.

They are an Antaean people, adamantine, indomitable, and profoundly certain of themselves. They are a natural people who have not lost, as we have lost, consciousness of unity with the natural world around them. They are an extraordinarily conscious people imbued with an exceptional sensitivity toward each other. They are a people who accept hardship and who, from the crucible of their endurance, had created the conditions requisite to human happiness. They are supremely effective human beings; and they are among the last inhabitants of this planet who still appear — or until recently appeared — to possess the answer to that nagging question, "Who, and what, am I?"

But this was an illusion. In distantly envisaging these peoples' lives as they had been, we failed to glimpse the heart of darkness beating black within the present hour. Their lives had undergone a sinister sea-change. We had not long been about our task when we began to recognize the change, and began to understand that our account was being transmuted, without our volition, into a requiem. We who had come to chronicle human life in its most admirable guise remained to witness and record the passing of a people.

And so the portrait we had planned was never made. The mood was altered irretrievably, and our book now tells a different tale.

In defence of the way of life of a people who have been dispossessed, in support of their right to that life and of the virtues inherent in it, we might have chosen to portray them in the happiest of circumstances and in the most favourable conditions — perhaps in the easy days of summer against the rippling colours of a land whose beauties are unique. We did not so choose because we believed, and we believe, that the essential qualities of these people need no gilding to establish their validity. And so, instead, we have portrayed them in the context of their world in its grimmest and most formidable aspect, in the hard, bleak days of winter.

It is surely an appropriate choice, since the portrait that we offer is of a people in the winter of their time.

Newfoundland is of the sea. Poised like a mighty granite stopper over the bell-mouth of the Gulf of St. Lawrence, it turns its back upon the greater continent, barricading itself behind the three-hundred-mile-long rampart that forms its hostile western coast. Its other coasts all face toward the open ocean, and are so slashed and convoluted with bays, inlets, runs, and fiords that they offer more than five thousand miles of shoreline to the sweep of the Atlantic. Everywhere the hidden reefs and rocks (which are called, with dreadful explicitness, "sunkers") wait to rip the bellies of unwary vessels. Nevertheless these coasts are a true seaman's world, for the harbours and havens they offer are numberless.

Until a few generations ago the coasts of the island were all that really mattered. The high, rolling plateaus of the interior, darkly coniferous-wooded to the north but bone-bare to the south, remained an almost unknown hinterland. Newfoundland was then, and it remains, a true sea-province, perhaps akin to that other lost sea-province called Atlantis; but Newfoundland, instead of sinking into the green depths, was somehow blown adrift to fetch up against our shores, and there to remain in unwilling exile, always straining back toward the east. Nor is this pure fantasy, for Newfoundland is the most easterly land in North America, jutting so far out into the Atlantic that its capital, St. John's, lies six hundred miles to the east of Halifax and almost twelve hundred miles east of New York.

Thousands of years ago Newfoundland was over-mastered by a tyranny of ice. Insensate yet implacable, the glacial presence crept out of Labrador, flowing from the northwest toward the southeast across the spine of the peninsula; arming itself with the jagged shards of mountains it had crushed in its inexorable passage. Bridging the narrow Straits of Belle Isle it engulfed the island. Great, tearing granite teeth, embedded in the ice, stripped the living flesh of soil and vegetation from the face of Newfoundland and gashed gigantic furrows in the underlying rock. The mountains of the interior were ground down to form a vast and almost featureless plateau, a realm of utter desolation. When the ice reached the southern coast, which in those times presented a mountain wall to the sea, it slashed a series of immensely deep wounds in the fronting cliffs, wounds that eventually became the fiords of southern Newfoundland.

With the island vanquished, the ice moved on to engage the sea itself in a titanic struggle. It thrust outward from the southeastern shores, forcing the waters back, until its invading snout extended three hundred miles to seaward. This was no superficial conquest: the glacier was a solid entity resting upon the ocean floor hundreds of fathoms down; and its ice-valleys and ice-mountains lay glittering beneath an arctic sky.

The waters were forced to retreat for perhaps a thousand years before the last ice-age approached its end. Then the sun burned with renewed passion and the congealed surface of the northern seas softened and reliquified. Illimitable ocean began to eat into the cold invader. The glacier, at bay, could not retreat as the sea had done; it could only stand and die. In death it delivered itself of billions of tons of soil and pulverized rock stolen from the land. This debris sank to the sea floor, where it remains as the vast area of shoal banks, including the Grand Bank of Newfoundland, fringing the southern and eastern coasts of the island of whose substance the banks were formed.

So the ice rotted from the sea and left the sea unmarred. But when it melted from the land it left the island scarified, denuded, a polished and eroded skull. Life crept back upon that bared bone with infinite slowness for, although the glacier itself was gone, the shadow and the influence of the vanished ice remained. Out of the polar seas flowed, and flows still, an arctic river called the Labrador Current. Sweeping down out of Baffin Bay and Hudson Strait, it chills the shores of Labrador and Newfoundland and, for several months of every year, wraps much of the island in the frigid embrace of drifting arctic ice.

The polar pack and the polar current are brutal adversaries of all life upon the lands they touch; but life on the coasts of Newfoundland, particularly on the Sou'west Coast, must also endure other inimical influences. One of these is the fog that in spring and summer can shut off the light of the sun for weeks on end. Then there is the wind. Raging unchecked across an unbroken sweep of water stretching to South America, out of the cyclonic cauldron of the Caribbean, come some of the world's most majestic and consuming storms. The south coast of the island lies full across their track; and from September through to May the furious winds seldom rest. The tortured air clamours against the sea-cliffs, driving the salt storm-wrack far inland as the winds scythe on toward the stony highlands of the interior, where only crawling, clinging vegetation can maintain its hold.

The Sou'west Coast is not, and has not been since before the ice-ages, a world hospitable to men who must make their living from the land. Before the coming of Europeans, even the native Beothuk Indians eschewed the Coast except during a few weeks in summer; then they crossed the tundra barrens from the wooded highlands far to the north and visited the shore to make a hurried harvest of sea birds, eggs and shell fish. The Beothuks hovered on the edge of the sea, at the brink of the vital discovery that it was the sea and not the land which was the key to human occupation of the Sou'west Coast. But the discovery itself was not for them to make since they were not truly a people of the sea.

Yet the very factors which turned this coast into a wasteland were, paradoxically, the factors which created the conditions for a rich and rewarding way of life for men: the surrounding waters. The glacial ice, which turned much of the high plateau into sub-arctic barrens, created the offshore banks which became the greatest fish pastures in the world. The cold Labrador Current paralyzed the coasts it touched, but produced simultaneously on the banks ideal conditions for the unbelievably fecund proliferation of living things.

After the passing of the glacier, life exploded in the offshore waters. The minute plankton animals and plants formed a veritable soup through which swam, fattened, and spawned untold numbers of fish of innumerable species. At the surface, horizon-filling flocks of sea-fowl fed on small fry and, with their guano, began the slow process of restoring life-conditions to the denuded islands and the bleak sea-cliffs. Millions of pelagic seals came drifting south early each spring to whelp on the pack-ice and feed their young high over the teeming fish life of the Banks. Pods of great whales, in numbers that may never have been equalled in the world's seas, lazed along the sweep of high and rocky coast. Seals invaded the bays and the shallow, sandy lagoons; otters appeared along the tide water; salmon began to re-enter the almost sterile rivers. Lobsters, mussels, winkles, and crabs returned to the shore rocks; and wavering jungles of kelp began to lift above the inshore reefs. And so it went, until the entire infinitely varied world of life within the sea was re-established, but on a vastly expanded scale, around the island mass which itself had hardly begun to be reclaimed by living things.

Life within and on the sea was the key to human life upon the coasts, the key with which to open the rock-ribbed island casket; but this key could only be grasped by men who were truly of the sea.

As the first such voyagers, sailing from European shores, approached the Sou'-west Coast, they saw from afar a looming wall of rock rising as much as a thousand feet out of the sea-foam; a forbidding granite wall which, at first sight, must have appeared totally inhospitable to mariners and ships.

With trepidation they ventured closer, the lead swinging steadily and the helmsman ready at a moment's notice to put about for the safety of the open sea. But they found a bold coast – "bold water," seamen call it – offering a deep and secure passage almost to the shoreline. And as they came under the loom of the sea-cliffs they saw that the apparently unbroken wall had many doors. Every few miles a fiord-mouth opened, sometimes as narrow as a knife-wound, sometimes wide enough to admit a dozen ships sailing abreast.

La Poile, Le Moine, Connoir, Bay de Loup, White Bear, Bay de Vieux, La Hune, Avalon, Chaleur, Facheux, Bay d'Espoir – all these and more slice into the coastal escarpment for distances of up to thirty miles. They are sheer-walled and possess a massive grandeur; but all of them hold inner nooks and coves where a vessel can anchor or moor right to the rock walls, in absolute security from any hurricane that ever blew.

At the heads of these great fiords white rivers, highways for the salmon, roar down off the interior plateau through deep and twisting gorges which, protected from the eternal winds, have clothed themselves in pine and spruce, hemlock and birch. The river-mouths are places where men can build cabins secure from the fury of the roiling winter seas and the spume-laden gales, with abundant firewood easily at hand; and where the gorges provide steep stairways up to the lip of the plateau to the caribou country where a man can still kill a winter's meat in a single day. So attractive were these inner sanctuaries that it became the pattern for early settlers to build "winter houses" in them to which they could retreat during the most violent months when fishing from frail open boats had to be abandoned temporarily.

But although the fiords offered a temporary shelter for ships and a retreat from the worst days of winter for the settlers, they were not places where many men could hope to build a permanent way of life. The key to human existence on the Sou'west Coast remained in the seas' keeping; and perforce, men had to make their real homes hard by the unquiet waters.

Perhaps no other ocean emanates such a disturbing feeling of sentience as does the North Atlantic. It is not just a realm of water, it is a veritable presence – one of incalculable moods. It is seldom still; even in its rare moments of brooding calm, a long and rhythmic swell rolls under the surface so that it ripples like the hide of a monster. It is at times like these that men of the sea distrust the sea most. They view the quiet interludes with foreboding; "weather breeders" they call such days, and they prepare for what they know will follow: a passionless and almost inconceivable violence of wind and water.

For those who live by it and upon it, the sea is the ultimate reality in their existence. They accept it as their master, for they know that they will never master it. The sea is there. It is their life: it gives them life and sometimes, in its moments of fury, it gives them death. They do not struggle against its imponderable strength, nor do they stand in braggart's opposition to its powers.

"Ah, me son," a schooner skipper told me once, "we don't be takin' nothin' from the sea. We sneaks up on what we wants – and wiggles it away."

WE SNEAKS UP ON
WHAT WE WANTS—AND
WIGGLES IT AWAY

T

his island was a reality in the conscious-
ness of European men long centuries before the void of darkness obscuring
the rest of the Western Hemisphere began to be filled with knowledge. It
was a concrete reality to Greenland Norse settlers who saw it first in 987, who
tried and failed to colonize it at the turn of the first millenium and called it
Vinland. It was an indisputable reality to the wide-ranging seamen of the
Basque provinces of Spain and France who whaled along its shores at least a
century before Columbus sailed west to immortality. By 1436 it had appeared,
if dimly, on European maps as The Land of Stockfish. Well before the end of
the fifteenth century Portuguese seamen knew it as Terra de Los Bachalaos;
Breton and Norman fishers knew it as Terre-Neuve; Bristol fishermen were
seeking it under a name whose origins are now lost to us – The Isle of Brasile –
and, on reaching it in 1481, adopted the French name and called it New Land.

Men of ancient centuries, fishing at great distances in time and space
from their home ports, had needs that only solid land could satisfy. There was
the need to shelter from the great Atlantic storms; the need for snug harbours
where ships could water, repair, and take on wood for fuel. Stockfish (dry
cod), whether it was preserved with salt or only dried by wind and sun, could
only be "made" on shore. The blubber from whales and seals could only be
"tried" (rendered into oil) at crude factories constructed on the land. Thus it
is certain that from the first days of the fisheries off Newfoundland men were
making at least seasonal use of the coasts. Skippers who came back year after
year – and many did – had their chosen harbours where permanent structures
came into being. Inevitably the owners had to take measures to protect their
shore-bases, not so much against the presence of the native Beothuks (who
were an inoffensive people), as against the thievery and malicious destruc-
tion by crews of other ships of their own and foreign nations.

The only certain way to protect a shore-base was to leave men to winter
there; and with the first such successful winterings-over, well before the end
of the fifteenth century, the seeds of permanent occupation of these coasts
were sown.

It was a short further step to the decision by certain hardy men to "plant"
themselves in New Land. The advantages were obvious: a group of men, per-

manently established in a convenient harbour, near good fishing grounds where they could use small boats, could fish for eight months of the year off the northern coasts and almost year-round off the southern shores.

There was more to settlement than that. During the early centuries of Newfoundland's discovery and occupation, the common man in Europe was in peonage – if not in outright bondage. His very, life was forfeit at the whim of those who governed him. The poverty of the damned was the general lot of most except the upper ranks. The hardships and uncertainties of hacking out a free life on the granitic coasts of Newfoundland were no greater than those a man had to face at home in Europe and, in all likelihood, were considerably less. And in Newfoundland, as in no other part of North America, there was only the natural hostility of wilderness with which to deal: the Beothuks made no real effort to resist the alien interlopers, as did their brothers on the continental mainland.

One thing was needed before the slow swirl of Europeans along the Newfoundland shores could begin to clot into real settlements – and that was women. Historians say nothing about where the women came from, but come they assuredly did. In the beginning some were taken forcibly out of the tents of the Beothuks. Others accompanied the fishing ships from Europe. The latter were women without homes, without men to keep them – women who perforce kept themselves the only way they could. Aboard ship they served the dual purpose of entertaining the crew and, in their spare time, slaving at the job of making fish. It cannot be doubted that, given an opportunity, those women would choose to abandon servitude in order to build a life with a free man, even in a remote cove in Newfoundland.

There is a legend (which is still perpetuated by some smug town-dwellers in Newfoundland) to the effect that the men and women who first settled the outports were criminals, outcasts and fugitives attempting to evade justice and punishment. This is a lie. Many of these people may have been law-breakers according to the oppressive regulations of their times; many of them certainly deserted from ships whose crews were treated little better than galley-slaves; others fled from a European justice so barbarous that it thought nothing of having a man drawn and quartered – but criminals they were not. They were in truth the strongest and bravest of the oppressed; and their only real crime was that they dared risk everything to gain the freedom to live or die by their own efforts.

The birthdate of the first real settlement on the Sou'west Coast is unknown. Written history holds no record of it, for it was not established with great fanfare by some aristocrat intent on building an empire in the new world. But although the Basque peoples of the fifteenth century left no documentary record of their distant venturings, Spanish scholars two hundred years later chronicled a Basque tradition which stated matter-of-factly that their seamen had been whaling off Newfoundland a full century before Columbus sailed. So it could well be that these mysterious and incredibly ancient people provided the Sou'west Coast with its first European inhabitants; and it is surely no mere coincidence that the harbour which is now Newfoundland's navel, and which lies at the western extremity of the Sou'west Coast, still bears the name Port-aux-Basques.

The first documented reference to settlement comes from the Portuguese. It is a fragmentary notice of a voyage made just before 1500. After this date the pattern becomes a little clearer. Until about the middle of the sixteenth century Portuguese, French and Spanish Basques, and Normans and Bretons were almost equally numerous and had together sometimes as many as six hundred ships in Newfoundland waters in any given year, mostly on the southern and eastern coasts. The Portuguese and the Spanish Basques seem to have occupied the Sou'west Coast under a rough and ready *modus vivendi* which gave the French (Bretons, Normans, and French Basques) possession of the remainder of the south coast, from Fortune Bay east to Cape Race.

As the years slipped by, Basque and Portuguese interest and influence in southern Newfoundland declined while those of the French grew. This shift was a continuous one – not a simple replacement of one people by another. Those early settlers who were already established when the French drifted westward remained where they were and blended their blood with that of the newcomers, eventually adopting the French tongue as the general language. The change was slow, spanning most of the seventeenth century.

In the train of the French came a new infusion of Indian blood. Micmacs of Nova Scotia, close allies of the French, were encouraged to migrate to Terre-Neuve, where they found no colour bar. Whites and Indians intermarried freely and lived and worked on a basis of equality.

Thus by the early eighteenth century the Sou'west Coast was home, and had been home for centuries, to a people of mixed Basque-Norman-Breton-Portuguese-Indian heritage. The race – and it was in reality a race – took on further admixtures, for during most of the seventeenth century this was a famous pirate-coast where Dutch, English, and Spanish freebooters made their headquarters secure from interference, since not even France attempted to exercise effective sovereignty over it.

The Sou'west Coast developed and preserved a remarkable degree of freedom from involvement in the wars, skirmishes, and raids that grew out of the bitter, decades-long struggle between France and England for possession of Newfoundland and Canada. It became and remained a neutral zone, bypassed by the warring fleets but visited by peaceful fishermen and honest pirates with profit to themselves and to the inhabitants. In consequence of this continuing freedom both from war and from official interference, the little clusters of families that now inhabited every suitable cove and harbour from Cape Ray to Fortune Bay developed no real sense of allegiance to any European nation. They were a people united within themselves in a society that had no name, no flag, no boundaries. The sea was their common country, and the way of the sea was their community of life. Each outport lived not only in freedom from the turmoil of the outer world but also in freedom from too-close propinquity even to its neighboring settlements, since each group of human beings in its cliff-girt cove was insulated from all other settlements by the dark wastes of ocean. Nevertheless the coast-dwellers were all as one people, for the sea had made them one.

Through the generations changes came imperceptibly to the coast, though in the main these changes were superficial and did not deeply affect the lives men led. Even the Treaty of Utrecht, in 1713, by which France was forced to cede the whole south coast to England, caused no severe dislocation of the centuries-old way of life. The English sent a naval officer, Capt. Taverner, to cruise the newly acquired coast and to demand an oath of allegiance from the settlers on pain of expulsion if they refused. He met with little if any resistance. The people took the oath. After all, what was a nominal change of allegiance to them? They went on about their age-old business with the sea.

But change in an unpleasant guise was on its way, with the arrival of carpetbaggers representing powerful merchant companies based in Southern England and in the Channel Isles. These newcomers seized some of the best harbours and proceeded to introduce the same mercantile system under which outport fishermen in the English parts of Newfoundland (the English had settled the East Coast as early as 1600) had been mercilessly exploited for generations. These merchants controlled all imports, and sold supplies on credit to the outport people to carry them through the next season's fishery; but they demanded exclusive rights to the fishermen's catch to be applied against their debt. If there was a surplus to the fishermen's credit (and the merchant was the sole judge of this, since the people were completely illiterate), it could only be "taken up in trade" at the merchant's store. The outport men were no longer allowed to sell fish to visiting ships of English or foreign nationalities, or to buy goods from them.

This system, once established, continued in full force until the 1940's, and is still in effect in at least one outport on the Sou'west Coast today. The profit on goods sold to outport fishermen sometimes exceeded five hundred percent, while the net profit on salt fish taken from them regularly amounted to three or four times the sum credited to the fishermen's accounts.

The arrival of the English and Jersey merchants had yet another result. These companies used indentured labour. Each year their ships brought out cargoes of so-called "youngsters" (men ranging in age from fourteen to sixty years) recruited mostly in the counties of Devon, Dorset, and Somerset and on the island of Jersey.

These "youngsters" were obliged to serve their masters for a period of from three to five years in exchange for their keep; and, if the masters so chose, they were obliged to make a payment of three or four pounds at the termination of the indenture. They were used as crews for the fishing boats owned by the merchants, and as brute labour; and sometimes they were hired out to English entrepreneurs who had established themselves as masters of certain small outports which they ran as minor principalities. Hundreds of the "youngsters" reached the Sou'west Coast in the eighteenth and nineteenth centuries, and few ever returned, or even wished to return, to the starvation lot of the poor in the England of those times. Some served out the full indenture period and then slipped away to take up the outport way of life. A great many others drew the breath of freedom early and ran off to hide themselves in bays and inlets where they too became "livyers" (people who "live here").

Chauvinistic historians have claimed that after Utrecht the French mysteriously vanished from the coast, to be magically replaced by an entire English population. Nothing of the sort occurred. The steady intermarriage of Englishmen with local girls gradually brought about an apparent anglicization of the population – a further extension of the melding process that initially made the south-coast people what they were. The language changed and the surnames of many families were anglicized. But other things did not change. Most of the old names for the bays, the settlements themselves, mountains, and rivers remained, as indeed they still remain. And the pattern of the coast-dwellers' lives did not undergo any essential change.

English officialdom showed little interest in the Sou'west Coast, leaving it to be run as a fiefdom by the great merchant companies whose only real opposition came after 1800 when Americans from New England began fishing the coast in earnest. In 1818 a treaty between Britain and the United States not only gave the Americans the right to fish the Sou'west Coast in any way they chose, but also allowed them to make use of any "unoccupied" harbours, creeks, or bays. This treaty remained in force for almost one hundred years.

The Americans' freedom to come and go as they pleased (a freedom shared, illegally, by the French fishing fleets operating out of the nearby French islands of St. Pierre and Miquelon) was bitterly resented by the English merchant companies. But it was a blessing to the people of the Coast: it offered them an escape-door, no matter how narrow, from complete servitude to the merchants. They could and did engage in an illegal bait-trade, selling squid and herring to American and French fishing vessels and getting paid in gold. And they could and did engage in an equally illegal trade with

St. Pierre and Miquelon, smuggling loads of lumber, fresh caribou meat, and other produce to the French islands – where they bought rum, sugar, flour, clothing, and similar essentials at a fraction of the price charged them by the merchant monopoly on their home coast. American vessels harbouring on the Sou'west Coast bought fur and fish from the local people, again for gold, and sold them cheap New England goods, while the merchant princes raged and sent delegation after delegation to England demanding that this poaching on their preserves be stopped by force.

Without the presence of the "foreigners," life on the Sou'west Coast might have become intolerable. For centuries the Coast people had endured adversity, had overcome and thrived on it; but that had been natural adversity. The ruthless exploitation (there is no other word for it) they had to endure under the rule of the English and Jersey merchants strained the fabric of their lives to the breaking-point. It became nearly impossible for a man to obtain or cling to much more than a fingerhold on existence. It became virtually impossible for the population to grow either in numbers or in spirit. Conditions grew worse in the first decade of the twentieth century, when the merchants at last succeeded in persuading the government to cut off the American trade. Left with a free hand, the merchant companies and the smaller independent merchants tightened their grip to such an extent that they very nearly throttled the life out of the Sou'west Coast. These were the years that are still starkly remembered by the old people as The Hard Times. And they were hard indeed. Starvation was a constant spectre. Malnutrition was something men were born to and died of. It is perhaps the surest measure of the qualities of the Coast people that they survived this period at all. They were helped by the two world wars which brought so much prosperity to the fishing business that a little of it managed to spill over from the merchants' grasp, and the people could draw new breath. After 1933, the new colonial government (a Commission established by Great Britain after Newfoundland's merchant princes had run the island into bankruptcy) began to offer help to a forgotten people. Cottage hospitals were built, and a free medical service (even if of a rudimentary nature) was provided. It was little enough help, but by the time the Second World War began, the people were on their feet again. True, the merchants still dominated the scene, but their grip had slackened sufficiently so that life could renew itself.

In the last hours before confederation with Canada became a reality, in 1949, the Coast was a land of vigorous men and women. They were a unique and fascinating breed. They were quick, confident, eminently successful survivors of an evolutionary winnowing-process that few modern races have undergone. As fishermen they were unparalleled. As seamen who had been manning ocean-going sailing ships for centuries, they were unsurpassed. Although their homes were remote from the outer world, they were by no means isolated in thought or in experience. There was hardly a family that had not sent sons, brothers, uncles, and fathers abroad as seamen or as skippers in the great overseas carrying-trade that before the Second World War had made the Newfoundland mercantile fleet one of the largest (in numbers if not in tonnage) in the world. London, Lisbon, and Genoa were names familiar in the mouths of most of the coastal peoples. Nor did they obtain their information about foreigners and foreign lands at second hand. Under-educated and largely illiterate as they may have been, their under-standing of and empathy with strange peoples with strange ways was deeper and embraced more tolerance than most of us can claim today.

The Islanders were always much more closely linked to the seaboard peoples of Europe than to those of North America. Until two decades ago they had no real political, little social and cultural, and not even much commercial affiliation with this continent. In 1867, when confederation with Canada was first mooted, Newfoundlanders lustily sang this song:

> *Hurray for our own native land, Newfoundland!*
> *Not a stranger shall hold an inch of her strand.*
> *Her face turns to Britain, her back to the Gulf.*
> *Come near at your peril, Canadian Wolf!*

And they were still singing the same song when Confederation came upon them.

The man who engineered Confederation was Joseph Smallwood, once a labour organizer and once a pig farmer, but always and forever a political animal; combining messianic visions with the essential ruthlessness of an Alexander, or a Huey Long. He became the first premier of Canada's newest province in 1949, and still remains its premier after a reign of nineteen years. "King Joey," as he is called (sometimes affectionately, sometimes with bitter-ness), has tried to transform his island kingdom into an industrialized principality, dependent on and imitative of the Admass society of Canada and the United States. "Off with the old and on with the new" is his guiding principle, and he has applied it with a vigour and a haste that have made no reckoning of the psychic and spiritual havoc it has created in the lives of his own people.

The day that Smallwood came to power, the continuity and evolution of the Newfoundland way of life was disrupted, probably forever. Newfound-land turned its back upon the sea which had nurtured her through five centuries. Fishing and fishermen, ships and seamen became obsolete. Progress, so the new policy dictated, demanded the elimination of most of the thirteen hundred outport communities that encircled the island, and the transforma-tion of their people into industrial workers. Progress dictated that the men of the sea forswear their ancient ways of life and move, as rootless migrants, to the alien milieu of industrial and mining towns. The entrepreneurs of the new industries wanted abundant labour and, of course, they preferred it cheap. The outport people had to be induced – and if not induced, then forced – to abandon the ways and the world they knew.

The tactics used combined both methods. The first step was to wither the fisheries and the mercantile marine by witholding the support which would enable them to make the transition into effective economic enterprises of the twentieth century. With their underpinnings knocked out the outports began to totter; but they did not fall, for their intrinsic strength was greater than the politicians had anticipated. The next step was to reduce basic services, or to fail to maintain them in the outports at a level comparable to that available to citizens in the factory towns. Outport schools found they could no longer obtain teachers; those regions (like the Sou'west Coast) whose main communications were by sea, found that the government-owned steamer-service was deteriorating. But the heaviest pressures were brought to bear through reduction in medical services. On the Sou'west Coast many outports found themselves going without a visit from a doctor for as much as ten months at a time, even though two government doctors were resident on the Coast and could call on helicopters and float-planes with which to reach the settlements.

In conjunction with these "deprival tactics" the government devised a centralization plan. Outporters were to be subsidized into moving to a few chosen "growth centres" on the coasts. At first people were offered $500 per family, provided that every family in an outport agreed to move. The size of this "assistance grant" has since been substantially increased, but it still falls far short of compensating the people for their abandoned houses, or for the cost of buying or building new homes in the chosen towns.

Whatever the tactic used, the aim itself is dubious in the extreme. The *raison-d'être* for the centralization plan is to create viable new economic and social units. Yet Burgeo, a typical growth centre on the coast, has suffered a massive expansion in its population without any increase in ways to provide it with a decent way of life. The one fish-processing plant in the town employs only a fraction of the employable people already living there, and it pays them only minimal and intermittent wages. Many of the younger men can find work neither at the plant nor on the fish company's ships, and are forced to seek work as far away as central Canada. Those fishermen who are determined to stick to the sea receive almost the same price for their fish today that they did fifteen or twenty years ago. Burgeo is not a growing community; despite its increase in size, it is a dying community; and it may be that this too is part of the plan, for a people once uprooted can more readily be forced to move again.

The heritage of the outport people at the time of Confederation held a promise for the future – a promise that a strong, venturesome, and viable people could move into our modern world with no loss of their own sources of strength, and perhaps with a great gain to the waning strength of other men elsewhere. It was a promise that had little or no meaning to the apostles of instant change.

I remember a summation of the outport people made to my wife and myself by a woman doctor, an employee of the new government who held a most responsible position on the Sou'west Coast. We were aboard the coastal steamer as she nosed into Burgeo harbour. The steamer blew a long and lugubrious blast on her whistle and, as the sound echoed amongst the islands, men, women and children began to appear from the scattered houses and move toward the wharf. The doctor, standing beside us at the rail, gestured toward them: "These people are scum. They are descended from scum, and they are still scum."

But I also remember a stormy evening in February when John de Visser and I sat in the snug kitchen of a fisherman's home in the village of François. Present with us were three men, a woman, and a girl-child. John and I had spent most of the day photographing the men as they hand-lined for cod from dorys pitching in a gale of winter wind. Now the time had come for rest and talk. As had been the case during most of the evenings we spent along that coast, the talk ranged wearily over the problems of a people who had no future, of a way of life whose end could not long be postponed.

After a while there was silence; it was the silence of men who, for the first time in their lives and, perhaps, for the first time in the lives of their people, were experiencing the ultimate bewilderment that had come upon them with recognition of the truth that they were completely helpless to save themselves.

The woman brought a pot of fresh tea to the table where we sat and filled our mugs. As she returned to her seat by the stove to begin combing her daughter's hair, her husband broke the silence.

"It's been fine you came to visit us. I hopes your 'snaps' turns out just what you was after, and that you'll make a good voyage out of them – a prosperous voyage, you know. But still and all, I'm wondering could you, maybe, do one thing for we? Could you, do you think, say how it was with us? We wouldn't want it thought, you understand, that we never tried the hardest as was in us to make a go of things. We'd like for everyone to know we never would have left the places we was reared, but . . . we . . . was . . . drove!"

The last word burst into the quiet room with a terrible intensity. The little girl, who had been half-asleep as the comb slipped through her long dark hair, stared up at her father with astonished eyes.

He slowly lowered his head until he was looking with an unseeing gaze at the splayed hands with which he clutched the table-top before him. Unconscious of us all he spoke once more, no louder than the half-heard murmur of the black waters gentling the pilings of the landing stage outside the door.

"Aye Jesus, Jesus God, but we was drove!"

WE WAS DROVE

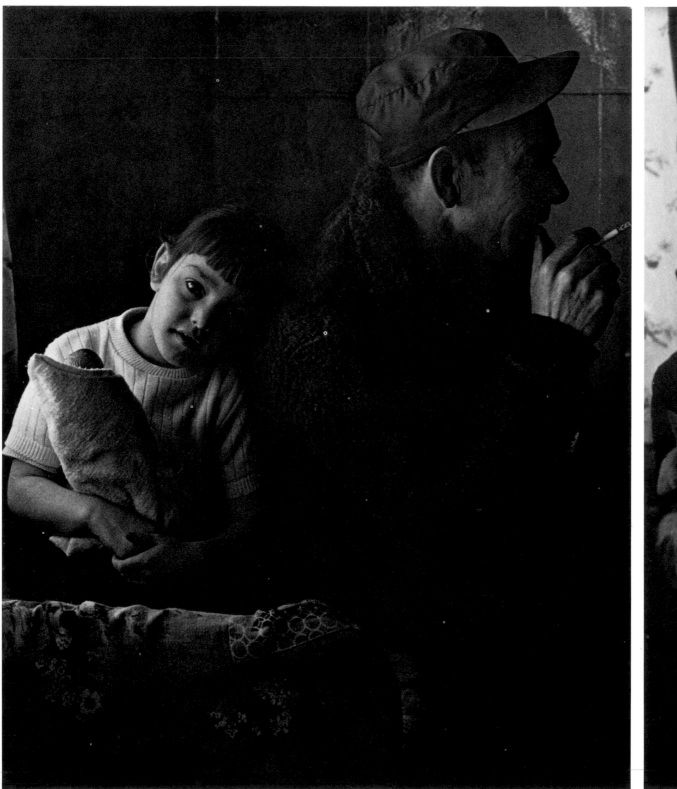

The brooding barrier of rock towering from the sea along the Sou'west Coast is kinder than it looks. It is pocked by scores of little coves (in addition to the fiords), some big enough to shelter a fleet of schooners and others only large enough to protect the boats and stages belonging to a handful of families. These were the places where men settled, always within a few hours' sail or row of good inshore fishing grounds.

There are fifty or sixty such coves along the coast, and hundreds of years ago they were all occupied. Together they formed a frieze of human habitations from Port-aux-Basques to Bay d'Espoir, along the line of demarcation between the surging sea and the rock ramparts. Their names sing a strange litany: Foxroost (it was once Fosse Rouge), Isle-aux-Morts, Rose Blanche (Roche Blanche), Harbour Le Cou, Petites, La Poile, Gallyboy, Grand Bruit, Our Harbour, Messers (Messieurs), Ramea, Burgeo, La Hune, Cul de Sac, François, Rencontre West, Dragon, Mosquito, Bonne Bay, Pushthrough, Goblin, Lobscouse Cove. But the song they sing is shorter now, and most of the coves have returned to silence.

Not all of the available havens were on the main shoreline. There was a scattering of bald-headed islands – indented with coves – all along the coast; and there was one remarkable archipelago embracing the Ramea, Burgeo, and Penguin island groups. By 1502 this archipelago was appearing on Portuguese charts as "The Islands Of The Eleven Thousand Virgins." Presumably it was so named by some devout master mariner in memory of Saint Ursula, the virgin martyr of Cologne; but the name may also reflect a sardonic seaman's humour, for when Don Jao Alvarez Fagundes officially claimed the islands for the King of Portugal in 1521, he noted dourly that they were uninhabited by men or women, virgin or otherwise; although they were surrounded by such an abundance of codfish that great fleets of ships resorted to them every year from Europe.

The Burgeo group huddles close up under the coast and was evidently settled soon after Fagundes' time. The Ramea Islands, five miles off shore (and originally called Ilos Santa Anna) apparently knew no permanent human inhabitants until a mere hundred and fifty years ago. The Penguins, a scattering of spume-swept islets fifteen miles off the towering headland of Cape La

Hune, were never permanently settled although families from La Hune and François summered on them until a few years ago, camping in makeshift huts and fishing for cod from two-man dorys. In times far removed the Penguins were the home of a vast breeding rookery of Great Auks. These huge, flightless birds furnished the transient fishing fleets and the local fishermen with countless tons of meat, most of which were used as bait, until the day came when the Great Auks could no longer withstand the slaughter and they disappeared forever from this earth.

Ramea and Burgeo are the two largest remaining settlements east of Rose Blanche; and the name Burgeo preserves the memory of the ancient Portuguese name for the archipelago, *Virgeones*.

Most of the early comers eschewed the naked islands and sought out sheltered coves on the main coast. The sites they picked were hardly determined by aesthetic factors (although many are spectacular in the extreme), nor for the creature-comforts they could offer; they were chosen solely because they were the best possible places from which to carry on the inshore fishery. Some – such as François, Richards Harbour, Cul de Sac, and Dragon – were built against such precipitous and rocky cliffs that there was hardly a square yard of level land to be found; and the houses clung precariously to steep, scree slopes, like so many seabirds' nests. At more exposed, if less rugged, coves the houses perched on spray-drenched foreshores of almost naked rocks behind which the small boats could shelter. These settlements had to withstand such ferocity of wind and water that the buildings were often bound to the rocks with ring-bolts and iron cables. Churches posed a special problem since anything that reached upward, whether toward God or an empty sky, was fair game for the wind. The Anglican church at Burgeo blew down three times in sixty years, with the result that not a few of the parishioners prudently transferred their allegiance to the Methodist faith. Burials posed a problem too. Often there was not enough soil in which to dig a grave, and thus the rough plank coffins had to rest on the surface rock, precariously protected for a few decades by mounds of peat and gravel.

It took indomitable persistence for an outport to root itself at all upon this coast, and everything about the surviving settlements bears testimony to this strength. The houses stand as square and solid as blocks of basalt. They are so strong that they can be levered off their foundation posts, trundled to the water's edge, set afloat, and towed miles across open water to be hauled up on shore at a new site – without suffering any damage in the process. When some of the outports were "closed out," the people refused to abandon their houses and shifted them in just this way. Scores of houses were "launched off," and one of the most remarkable sights I have ever seen was a flotilla of such houses being towed by a gaggle of little motor-boats. One house, whose lower rooms had been filled with oil drums to give additional buoyancy, carried the family as passengers in the upper storey. Its owners had even rigged the kitchen stove in one of the bedrooms, and the wife cooked lunch and "boiled the kettle" during the voyage.

Many of the coves were devoid of soil; but even that drawback could be, and was, overcome. Over the generations people patiently made things grow. They built potato patches by collecting baskets of detritus that had lodged in crevices amongst the rocks; and by manuring this sterile stuff with seaweed and rotting fish, they gave it a measure of fertility.

The wheel had little utility in most outports. The houses grew like barnacles, strewn every which-way among the boulders; and the paths that linked them were so steep and rough that, in many cases, even a wheelbarrow was of little use. That did not matter either. Strong arms, strong legs, and two-man handbarrows served the purpose of the wheel.

The settlements were not purely functional. It was a monochromatic world that the first settlers knew, but they gave it colour by planting seeds gathered in European gardens in centuries past. The cerulean iris (the *fleur-de-lis*), the wild briar rose, and other hardy, elder flowers adapted so well that many still persist at settlement sites from which houses and people have now vanished.

In the early times there was no paint to buy (supposing men had had the money with which to buy it), so that outporters made their own by mixing red ochre with cod liver oil. Although the resultant mixture stank to high heaven for a year or so, it gave warmth and colour to the buildings in the coves.

Until Confederation many families kept a cow and spent summer days gathering salt grass which grew in protected places, turning it into hay against the long, wild winters. Sheep and goats, which were imported so long ago that they developed into distinctive breeds, also learned to survive and even prosper where previously only caribou had been able to find sustenance. And then there were the dogs – the "water dogs" – black, smooth-haired beasts with massive forequarters, otter-like tails, and webbed feet – dogs almost as much aquatic animals as they were animals of the land. Nobody knows where they came from or when they came, but they seem to have been on the Newfoundland coasts when history first begins to speak about the island. It is from this aboriginal stock, remnants of which still exist upon the Sou'west Coast, that the famous breeds known as the Labrador and the Newfoundland were developed.

On a foundation of sterility and desolation the men and women of the coves built their small, strong worlds – bastions of courage and endurance wherein there dwelt a resolute and prideful race.

BASTIONS OF COURAGE
AND ENDURANCE
WHEREIN THERE DWELT
A RESOLUTE AND
PRIDEFUL RACE

In winter the small world of an outport appears to be sunk in somnolence, half-abandoned. Even on those days when no storm wraps the settlement in an obscurity of driving snow and spume, there is so little movement to be seen that a stranger might conclude that most of the inhabitants were hibernating. But this is an illusion. Within the narrow compass of the cove, "between wind and water" as the people say, life is being lived with undiminished vigour.

The cove comes alive well before dawn-light as the first fishermen board their boats and start their engines. The slow, heavy beat of the single cylinder "make-and-breaks" is a sound that is felt rather than heard, and it is the heartbeat of the settlements. Throughout the short day, life flicks its fingers intermittently across the cove. A dory dawdles in the narrow run between two islands as its owner hauls his herring nets. Someone is shovelling snow from the deck of a little schooner. There is always work to be done aboard the moored vessels – knocking off the ice after a "glitter" storm, pumping the bilges, replacing chafed mooring gear, or repairing a recalcitrant engine. The arena of the harbour is seldom crowded in the winter; but it is seldom empty.

It is the same along the landwash where men spend the balance of their lives when they are not at sea or in the home. The landwash is the indeterminate region where the water meets the land. It is a domain of docks, flakes, stages, fishstores, upturned boats, and tidal wrack. The skeletal structure of the "stages" (wharves) dominates the landwash, brooding over the scum of cat-ice that forms during the winter nights and breaks and flows away as the tide falls. Behind and often attached to each stage stands the fishstore, known simply as "the store," where gear is stowed, lines baited, nets repaired, boats built, and where, in the glow of a little stove, those who are too old or too young for the fishery foregather to wait until the boats come home from seaward.

Each man's store is each man's club. It is ill-lit and cluttered, redolent with the smells of stockholm tar, of salt bulk fish, of pickled herring, of old net twine, and of spruce sticks snapping in the stove. The store is a museum too, for it contains the memories of a man and of his fathers' fathers. Here, in dark corners, lie conch shells once used as foghorns; worn, red sealskin boots from Labrador; a broken "swile" (sealing) gun of gargantuan proportions; inscrutable objects of brass and copper that are the finite wreckage of some long-lost ship; a pair of homemade "racquettes" (snowshoes); and the phallic mass of an antique jump-spark engine that has not belched aloud for forty years. Men gravitate from store to store. A stranger may never see them either come or go, but if he pushes open the strap-hung door and steps inside he finds the club in session – if not in Garge's store, then sure to be in Sam's.

This is the place where the slow, casual gossip of the sea is heard – and old stories, sharp jokes, and subtle drolleries. And hands are always busy mending twine, baiting gear for the morrow's trip to the "grounds," playing the intricate cats-cradle known as "the schooner game" – doing a thousand things; for until the heart is stilled, the hands of an outport man are seldom idle.

The landwash embraces the steamer dock and, when the visiting ship lets go her long, evisceral rumble from outside the farthest headland, men, women, and children appear mysteriously, drifting down toward the dock. The crowd does not gather, it seems simply to grow and swell. The people stand about and watch the freight coming ashore. They gossip with passengers aboard the ship, exchanging news about old friends in other coves. They come to greet the steamer not out of idleness but to taste the continuity of life along the coast. The steamer is the link, not only between the outports, but to St. John's and to even more distant places in the outer world.

The houses crowd close to the landwash, and to one another, in a cheerful propinquity that owes nothing to the mathematical mind of a town planner. Their arrangement and alignment appears to be wildly haphazard; and so it is, if one thinks only of the neatly patterned and deadly-dreary streets of mainland towns. The pattern of an outport is not dictated by man; it is dictated by the vagaries of the riven rock to which the houses cling. This may be an offence to the eye of a planner, but the effect is a delight to the eye of anyone else, a delight that is enhanced by the boldly individualistic and lavish use of paint in wild and brilliant hues. The brash colours flow together in the random pattern of the buildings and, against the sombre backdrop of the winter cliffs, acquire beauty not by design but by happy accident.

Linked by a meandering web of pathways twisting and twining uphill and down, the houses with their gardens and wooden fenced enclosures form a different arena; but it too is seldom wholly empty, though seldom crowded. Children on their way to school run leaning into wind and driving snow; a woman emerges from her house and scuttles to the little merchant's store to buy a pound of salt pork. A brisk young man goes by, accompanied by his water dog hauling a country "slide" (sled) which carries a suspicious-looking lump of something, well wrapped in canvas, that may well be and probably is a quarter of illegal caribou meat. Old Uncle John swings past, on his way up from the landwash, a string of cods' heads, destined for his supper, bumping against his legs. Clem comes along the path to meet his cow who is waiting impatiently for her evening feed. Girls who have worked a long shift in the fish plant, red-faced and red-nosed in the evening chill, tramp wearily homeward. And all day long there is someone going to or coming from the well. Even when darkness falls, leaving each house alone but glowing outwardly through its frilled curtains, the slow and easy flow of human motion does not cease entirely. The lithe shadows of young people slip past and into greater darkness, melting and clinging as the night grows old.

The oil lamps burn in every kitchen, and the rank coal-smoke staggers from the chimney-tops as snow begins to fall, obscuring all the cove and waking the guardian fog horn on the outer head, so that its heavy voice begins to boom above the never-ending mutter of the sea; calling, calling into the black night; crying, "We are here. . . ."

CALLING, CALLING
INTO
THE BLACK NIGHT;
CRYING,
"WE ARE HERE…"

The home of an outport Newfoundlander is not the man's castle, it is the woman's. It is at once the core and the boundary of her existence. Once she has come to it as a bride, when she is perhaps no more than sixteen years of age, she rarely leaves it for more than a few hours, not because she is imprisoned in it but because for her it is the area of ultimate reality, the cave of ultimate security. Within these walls she becomes the mistress of her world, accomplished in a score of skills and unconsciously at ease in her fulfilment.

The outport house has evolved to suit its environment as surely as any animal evolves to suit its world. Built four-square, with the flexible strength that belongs to wooden ships, it makes total use of the space its walls enclose. The roof is pitched almost flat, since in this land of winds there is but little chance of its being overloaded with accumulated snow. The ceilings are low and heavily beamed, and the rooms have the snug and comfortable feeling of a vessel's cabin. Essentially the house is a land-berthed ship. Its upper deck contains the bedrooms, usually four in number, and unheated. Big beds – soft-sprung and mattressed with down ticks – almost fill them, for in these homes a bedroom is exactly what its name implies and nothing more. The lower deck may have a parlour and perhaps a bedroom too; but the main cabin is the kitchen, the heart and essence of the house.

The kitchen is the largest room; bright, warm, and welcoming. It always contains at least one "daybed" (a combination of sofa and single bed) which provides a place for the man to stretch out for a few minutes before his meal; a place for the woman to sit with the children beside her as she knits, sews, or spins; a place for a gaggle of neighbours' children to perch in owl-eyed silence; a place for a grandfather or an aging aunt to rest and reminisce; a place where young lovers come together when the rest of the household lies sleeping.

The stove is central and looms large; it glitters with nickel trim, and its top shines like a black mirror with the accumulated polish of the years. Above it hang thick woollen mittens, socks, children's outer clothing – all swinging and steaming. It is a room where everything is neatly in its place, ship-fashion; and it is kept scrupulously clean. The kitchen is colourful to such a degree that the eyes of a mainlander are dazzled by the brilliance of high-gloss paints upon the walls and by the gleaming, painted linoleum or canvas on the floors.

Not so long ago most of the furniture was hand-made, and well-made, by men who had acquired their competence as carpenters at the intricate work of ship-building. Today the pervasive influence of the mail-order catalogue has made its mark, but has not yet destroyed the aura of the outport kitchen.

The kitchen windows – there are usually two – look out upon the cove and over it to the grey sea beyond. During the long hours when the husband's boat is away at the fishing grounds, the woman's glance is forever reaching out beyond this room, so that the eyes of the house – the salt-streaked eyes of glass – become her eyes as well.

As for the man, he spends so little time in his own house that he sometimes seems to feel slightly uneasy in it. He often leaves it before dawn. If it is a good day, he may be at sea until late afternoon, after which he will be preoccupied at his stage or store until suppertime. On a "leeward day," when the weather "ain't fittin' " and the boats stay in the harbour, he spends most of his time down at the store. The house is where he eats his meals, sleeps, procreates, and occasionally indulges in some special skill – carving ship models, perhaps, or whittling out birch brooms. But it is only when he is very old, "not good for it anymore," that he at last enters fully into the house he built, or that his father's father built before him.

So the house belongs truly to the woman, and she gives of it to her children who are born within its walls; to young lovers; to her husband and to aged relatives; and, as often as circumstances will allow, to the entire settlement. There is no single thing in their lives that outport people value more than what they call a "time."

Almost anything will serve as an excuse to have a time and to fill the house with people. The arrival in the harbour of a fishing vessel from another port, a member of whose crew is perhaps a fifth cousin of some local householder, can spark a time. During the Twelve Days of Christmas (the outports still celebrate both old and new Christmas day and the twelve days between), every night is a time in its own right. Masked and costumed mummers come pounding at every door: "Is mummers allowed in?" Once inside they pound the kitchen floor with sea boots and rubber boots to the shrilling of a fiddle or the whine of an accordion. A time can happen quite spontaneously when three or four neighbours drop in for a "gam" (gossip), or it can be made to happen with the miraculous appearance of a bottle of "white stuff" (pure alcohol), imported without the blessing of the Customs Officer from the off-lying French islands of St. Pierre and Miquelon on foggy nights when the Royal Canadian Mounted Police patrol boats are drowsing at their moorings.

Here there is gaiety. But there is also pain and fear and darkness in the spirit. This is the place where women watch and wait through the interminable night, while the house shivers in the tearing talons of a winter's gale and a boat is too long overdue. It is the place where people sit in silence, but not alone, while in an upstairs room a pulse flickers fitfully and a heartbeat slows. The outport home rejects no man and no emotion. It accepts all that there is of life and death. It provides a place where those who have outworn their flesh can wait the hours down. For them there is no banishment to "a room of one's own," or to an old folk's sterile dying-place where they must endure that pervading chill of death, preceding death, that freezes the spirit of the world's unwanted. Until their last breath fails, those whose present has become their past are nurtured within the haven of these walls. And at the going out at the end of it they pass in dignity and in simplicity. And they are mourned.

Within these walls there is a sustaining certitude that is proof against disaster, against hardship, against the darkest hours of adversity, and against loneliness. Here there is a quality to human sharing, and an unspoken understanding that is proof against the very fates themselves. Here there is a unity that has no name. And here there is quiet at the close.

AND QUIET AT THE CLOSE

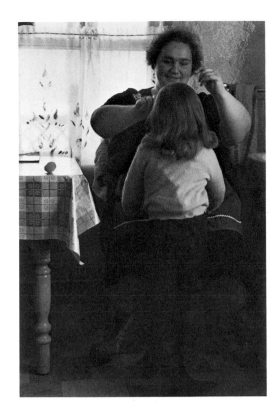
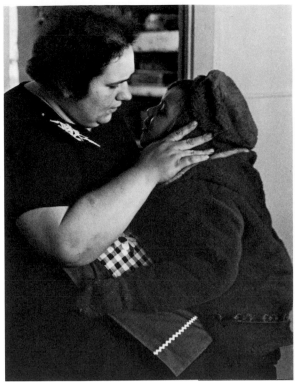

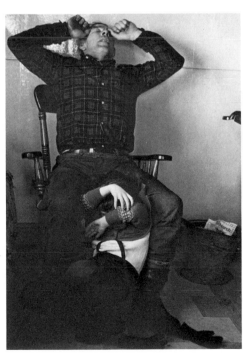

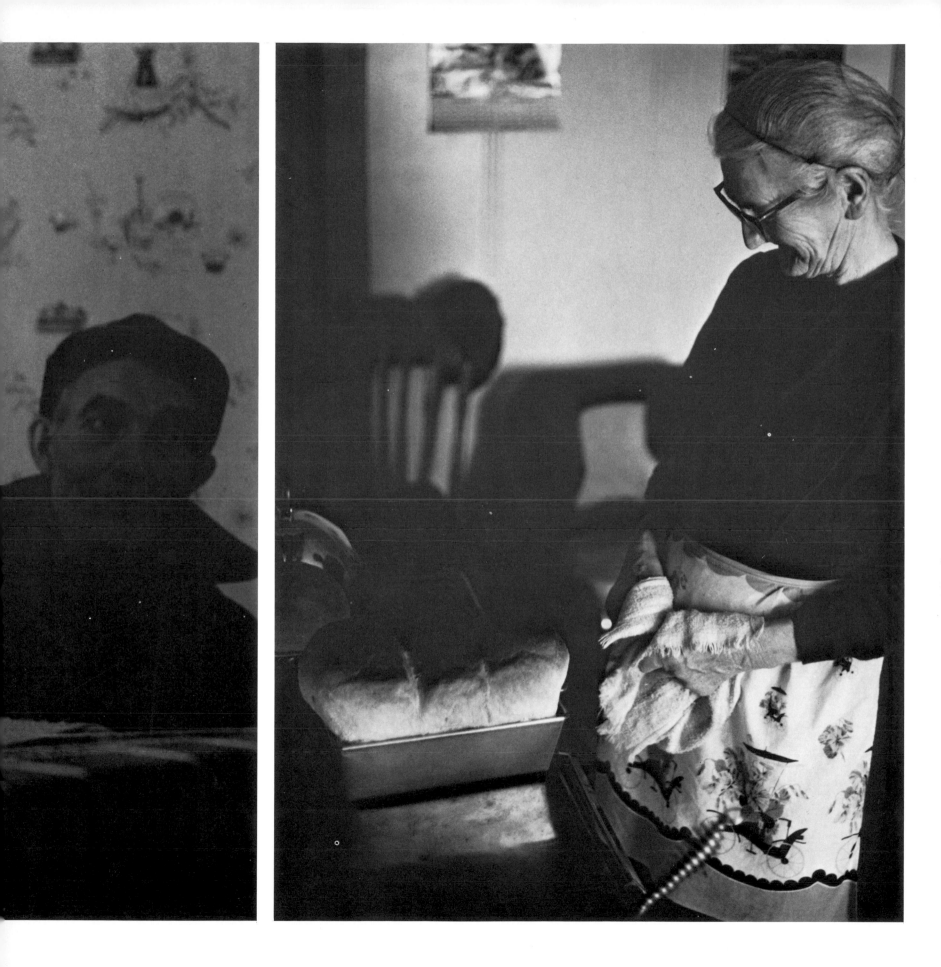

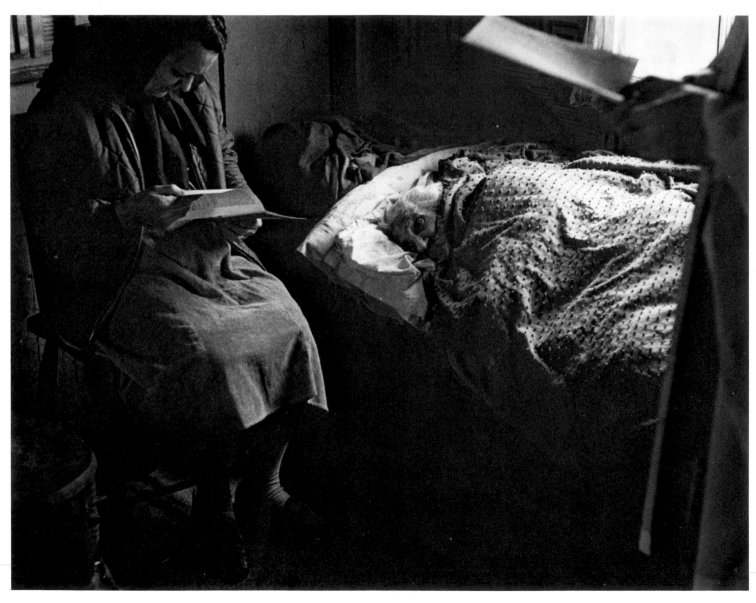

The world of the outport man is the
world of waters. He has eyes for little save the sea. His constant thoughts lie
with it. When he steps outside his door his glance lifts unconsciously toward
the sky, then drops to the line between sky and water, and finally interrogates
the face of the sea itself. Weather and water are preoccupations ingrained in
him since childhood. Like a true mammal of the sea, his real existence is
aquatic; all else is peripheral to him. Because he is truly of the sea, he does
not sentimentalize about it. He neither loves it nor hates it nor fears it; but
he holds it in abiding respect. And it is perhaps this respect, as much as anything, which gives him his innate and enduring respect for himself.

The world of waters is a complex one, even for those who go only on its
surface. Men from the outports may go as seamen on coasting vessels, aboard
an ocean-going tramp, on tugboats, on icebreakers or cable ships, or they may
go as fishermen in every kind of vessel from one-man dorys to giant new stern
draggers. They may even go afoot, upon the frozen world of the pack ice, as
the sealers go in the spring of the year.

Through the centuries, the pattern of their lives has changed; but the
change has been infinitely slow, and there is a recapitulation of the centuries
in the life of any outport man. As a child of three or four years he comes to
know the landwash, to recognize and be familiar with the sounds and smells
of the sea's edge in quiet and in storm. A year or two later he has found his
way to the stage-head where he will spend hours fishing for little tomcods or
trying to gaff flatfish. At seven or eight he goes with an uncle, or with his father,
in a dory to jig for squid; or perhaps to wade knee-deep in the breakers on
some gravel beach to dip up capelin in a wicker basket. By the time he is ten
or eleven, he will have his own lobster pots and will think nothing (nor will
his parents) of rowing singlehanded in a dory for several miles to jig for cod.
In winter he will join his fellows playing the dangerous game of "copying" –
leaping from floe to floe across the salt ice, as the grown man must do when
he joins the sealing ships. In late summer and early autumn the youngster
learns to make salt fish by helping members of his family split and salt a few
quintals (a quintal is 112 pounds) of cod – not to sell, but to eat at the family
table. By the time he is thirteen or fourteen, he has done almost all those things

which comprised the life of a fisherman on these coasts perhaps four centuries ago. The recapitulation is complete, and what began as pastimes have become the man's way of life; he has become one with the world of waters.

In the beginning the liveyers fished from small skiffs or shallops. The fish were "plenty" then. A man rowed or sailed his boat as much as fifteen miles to the best grounds, dropped a light anchor, and set about jigging to such effect that he would be knee-deep in fish by noon. Then he rowed home, gutted his fish, split it, salted it, and finished his work as the day finished. If he had a bumper catch, his wife and children would help him split and salt. During the day, if it was fine, the women spread the salt fish on the flakes to cure.

This was a way of life the antiquity of whose origins escapes the reach of our inquisitive probings into the past. The jigger, a decoy fish suspended by its snout with large hooks embedded in its tail, has a known history extending back for six thousand years. A version of it, cast in lead by fishermen of the North Sea two thousand years ago, is nearly identical with the leaden jiggers that are still being cast and used by the outporters of the Sou'west Coast in 1968.

Jigging was the way it was done in the beginning, and there are still a few old men who stubbornly retain it as their basic fishing method. But for most men it was long ago pushed into the background by the development of hand-lines. These consist of long, heavy lines to which "sudlines" (short leaders), each carrying a single baited hook, are fastened at intervals of a fathom. Working from a dory, two men can set several "tubs" (perhaps half-a-mile) of line, which is anchored and buoyed at both ends. When the line is all out, they return to the starting point to "haul their gear" and, with luck, may take a fish from almost every hook. "Fish," be it noted: in Newfoundland this word means codfish and nothing else.

With the beginning of hand-lining came the need for bait. During the course of the year a fantastic variety of bait is used as, when, and if it becomes available. Mussels and clams must serve when nothing else can be found. During the late winter and early spring the bait is herring, taken in shimmering thousands from nets off the headlands and in the runs between the islands. In early summer the capelin – small, sleek, brilliantly coloured little fishes – storm the beaches in untold millions to lay their eggs at the high-water mark. They too are bait. In summer the squid strike into the shore and men fill their dorys with them. Seine nets are used to catch the primitive sand lance. In older times sea birds, both young and old, were used extensively. Fishing for bait is in itself an important and highly specialized skill among Newfoundlanders.

Hand-lining lasted for centuries, and still persists. At François and a few other outports it is still the favoured method and is still done from two-man dorys. Incredible as it may seem to some of us, this is a matter of choice.

These men prefer the open boats, the heave and thrust of the great seas, the cut and slash of wind and spray.

One January day, when the temperature was down to 20 degrees and the salt spray froze on the oars and on the dory's gunwales, I went hand-lining with Uncle Tom, a man sixty years of age. For hours he worked his gear barehanded, while I huddled in the stern and slowly perished. When we got back to the cove that evening I was in a state of fury. "By God," I told him angrily, "it's bloody well inhuman for a man to have to get his living like this. It's a crime!"

Uncle Tom turned to me with mild surprise in his faded eyes. "Not human did ye say? Why, me dear man, 'tis the finest kind of life. Think of they poor fellows on the draggers now, gone from home a week and maybe two. But we'uns here gets home each evening, and there's the woman waitin' and the fire roaring up the stack. A crime you calls it?"

All the same, hand-lining is almost finished. It has been supplanted by long-lining, which is essentially the same method except that bigger, enclosed, and much more powerful boats are used. They carry crews of from two to eight, and they can work far out at sea, hundreds of miles from their home ports, setting miles of gear each day. They do well at it too. Two men in a small long-liner can bring in as much as four thousand pounds of fish a day when the fish are plenty; and if they received a fair price for their catch, they would make as good a livelihood as a man could wish for. But there's the rub. Cod, gutted and delivered to the door of the fish plant in Burgeo, may fetch no more than two and a half cents a pound, yet it sells to the consumer on the mainland for twenty times that price!

A low price for the catch is, and always has been, the basic handicap of the fisherman in Newfoundland. Before the Second World War, most of the offshore fishery (as opposed to the shore fishery carried on from small boats fishing close to home) was done by schooners equipped with fleets of dorys, owned and outfitted by large and small merchants and merchant companies. Men often went out for months aboard these vessels; they starved and froze and all too often drowned while hand-lining or jigging from open dorys far out of sight of land. If they survived they were lucky to get even a starvation wage. Nowadays diesel-powered draggers with huge otter trawls (big nets that are dragged along the bottom) catch whatever may be there and, in the process, rip up the spawning beds as well. Those few outport men who manage to get berths on the draggers, and who spend a week or ten days at a time at sea, can make a living – just. But their share of the returns is not even vaguely commensurate with the value of the catch. Life on a dragger is demanding and exhausting, yet this is not a matter for complaint. A mate from the Burgeo fleet described the draggermen's feelings in these words: "Nobody minds rough weather and hard times at sea. We're used to that. It suits us, you might say. Nobody stays ashore because of that. But times has changed, and these times people wants their fair and proper share. I'd never blame them if they stays ashore once they finds out there's nothing in it if they goes to sea."

The sea is the abode of riches, but precious little of that wealth rubs off on the hands of Newfoundland fishermen. It is a point the modern bureaucrats carefully avoid discussing when they cite the poverty of the outports as an excuse for closing them down. They would do well to remember and to admit what they know all to well: that this is the poverty of exploitation and not essential poverty at all. They would do well to alter the imbalance between the earnings of the fishermen and the earnings of the plant operators and middle-men, as a just and honest means of restoring the viability of the outports whose death they so blindly and callously seek. They would also do well to acknowledge another fact that is usually concealed: that the outports are not and never have been dependent on a single type of fishing operation. The truth is that the sea at their door offers the outport people a tremendous diversity of gainful work. Apart from the cod, redfish, sole, and haddock fisheries (which is where the interests of the big operators lie), the outport men can and do take halibut, herring, mackerel, turbot, swordfish, salmon, lobsters, shrimp, and sometimes seals as well.

However, the sealing game, once a great one in Newfoundland, is now almost at an end. Like so many other activities upon the sea at which Newfoundlanders were unexcelled, this too has been allowed to fade. Before Confederation thousands of men journeyed from all over the Island to the Avalon Peninsula each March to "muster" on the scores of sealing ships and steam off to the ice. The outports of the Sou'west Coast contributed their share of "swilers" (sealers) and the sealing brought in almost the only cash money that many Newfoundlanders ever saw. Six weeks of gory work upon the dangerous pack might net a man only fifty dollars in cold cash, but that was big money – although only a fraction of what the owners of the sealing ships realized from the work of the sealers. But now, in 1968, only one Newfoundland ship still goes to the ice and she carries a mere sixty swilers. A multi-million-dollar harvest has been abandoned to Norway and to Norwegian-controlled vessels sailing out of Halifax under the Canadian flag.

So much has been abandoned in the world of waters; and most outporters are fully aware of what has been taken from them. "St. John's just wants to clear us all out of it," a middle-aged fishermen in Ramea told me. "Little them fellows care if we has to leave all that's dear to us. Why don't they give us the chance to work here where we belongs? There's still plenty fish in the sea, and we're the byes could catch 'em if we had the half-a-chance."

There is no doubt that he is right. During the past eight years, I have visited comparable regions in Europe and in Asia that support small fishing communities whose problems of continuing survival parallel those facing the outport people of Newfoundland. I found that there had been no depopulation of those coasts. People who had always been fishermen and who wished to continue in that way of life had been given the chance to do so. In Norway, Iceland, the Faeroe Islands, Finland, and the U.S.S.R. it is government policy to provide meaningful assistance to the coastal dwellers so that they can make real progress toward achieving a good way of life compatable with modern standards, and in a manner of their own choosing. And this rational approach has brought big dividends to the nations concerned: their fisheries are now important economic assets; these countries have put themselves in the forefront of the harvesters of the oceanic farms to which we must turn with increasing need if we are to feed the human species and dispel the shadow of world starvation.

Newfoundland had the men. The men had the skill and the will. They lived poised on the very edge of the greatest fishing grounds in all the world. All the advantages were theirs – save one. Those who held their future in their hands turned contemptuously away from the world of waters. And so it is the fleets of other nations who today reap the harvest of the Newfoundland seas – fleets belonging to nations whose leaders could distinguish between the illusion and the substance of progress; to nations that gave their coastal people "the half-a-chance."

THERE IS STILL PLENTY
FISH IN THE SEA
AND WE'RE THE BYES
COULD CATCH 'EM

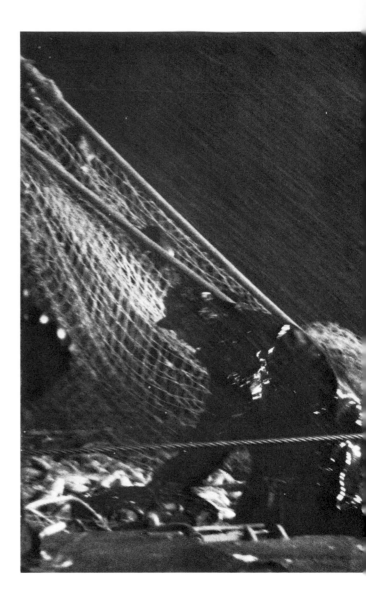

The world of waters always looms foremost in the men's minds, but the high plateau beyond the sea's reach also plays a part in the life of the outport people. From every settlement there is a trail leading inland. It is called the Country Path, a strangely gentle sobriquet for a track that may lead up a precipitous cliff face for a thousand feet; that can demand of the traveller that he use his fingers as well as his toes in order to navigate the crumbling, vertiginous ascent. The Country Path is not always an exercise in mountain climbing; from some outports it winds inland up the rocky pitch of a river valley; but it is always a hard road, and it leads into a hard land.

Nevertheless most outports held a few men who preferred the stark tundra plain to the rolling plains of ocean. These were mainly men who carried within them the instinctive predilections of Indian ancestors. Leaving the settlements in October, accompanied by their dogs and laden with all the supplies they could carry, they traversed the windswept sweep of the high barrens until they came to the southward edge of the Big Woods, the inland forest that lies forty or fifty miles to the north. Here they would build tiny cabins called tilts, and spend the winter trapping fox and wolf and mink and marten. They were seldom seen again until late February when they emerged from the wilderness with the season's catch. They were called "the countrymen," but now they are mostly gone, and those few who still survive are old men living with their memories.

The country still casts a lesser spell on almost every man in the outports, for at least a part of each year. In the past it was the country that gave them fresh meat, fuel for their hungry stoves, and wood with which to build their boats and homes and stages. Meat meant ptarmigan, hares, caribou and, in later years, moose as well; but caribou were by far the most important game. In the old days caribou roamed the winter barrens in "companies" of thousands. Those days are gone, and so are most of the "deer" slaughtered by commercial hunters who used to go out by the trainload from St. John's and intercept the herds as they migrated south across the railroad tracks. But small herds still remain; and the first heavy snows bring a restlessness to the outport men as their eyes turn briefly from the sea toward the land, and their thoughts go to the southward-moving herds. The caribou are forbidden to them now, by ukase of a government which wishes to reserve the remaining herds as targets for sport-hunting by wealthy mainlanders; but the peoples of the coves are not to be deprived so easily. On a December day when the west wind whips the snow into driving billows across the inland world, white-clad figures drift quietly out from amongst the houses and take the Country Path.

When they return, they do so in darkness; and the creak of the loaded slides on brittle snow is all that betokens their approach. In the morning, life in the outports goes back to its accustomed patterns; but the merchants note with disgust that for the next few weeks the housewives show remarkably little interest in purchasing salt beef or pork.

A HARD ROAD
INTO
A HARD LAND

However great may be the fears and doubts which now beset the men and women of the coves, however strained and tormented their dissolving lives become, they struggle with unyielding stubbornness to keep their children's lives inviolate for as long as possible. Although their own world is shrinking in upon itself as the peripheral defences fail, the outport men and women defend the inner citadel with a determination that is no less awe-inspiring because it is unconscious. This inner citadel is the world of children. Here, and here alone, the verities and certainties of the coastal people remain secure.

The children come and go in the shelter of their shielded world with casual insouciance. They lead their lives without being subjected to much more than token restraint imposed by their society. Nobody and no group takes it upon themselves to "organize" the children's lives. They go to school, but the school exists to teach them the essentials and not as an instrument intended to dominate their entire waking hours. The fact that most outport schools now fail in their primary purpose has no relevance to the freedom of the childrens' lives. Theirs is a truly "permissive" way. The rules they learn, and learn to follow, are mostly undefined. They are learned by a kind of osmosis, a soaking-in of what goes on around them. There is almost no aspect of the adult world of the outport from which the children are excluded and in which they cannot participate to some degree.

The children share a universal family. Almost every man and woman of middle age or more in the settlement is honorary aunt or uncle to every girl and boy. Each home is nearly as much the home of every child as is the one wherein he or she was born. The children circulate throughout the settlement as if they owned it all in common. Bevies of little girls, some of them barely old enough to walk, push open the door of any kitchen, slide silently in, and arrange themselves on the daybed where they sit and giggle and observe. Small boys haunt the stages, the boats, and the stores where they fiddle with the gear and listen to the unselfconscious talk of men, unwittingly absorbing the knowledge and the attitudes from which their fathers drew their enduring strength.

For the children it is all a game, yet it is playing at reality. They seem to play their youth away; and when they play amongst themselves they do so with an abandon and a zest which makes a stranger from the outer world feel sick at heart in the knowledge of how, all unknowing, he was cheated of the hours of his own childhood, and of how he has conspired to help cheat his own children of those hours.

The delights and satisfactions of childhood can only be fully realized where there is ultimate security and certainty; and the outport people still ensure that these conditions exist; and yet, because they do so, they are coldly condemned by the apostles of the New Life.

"These children," I was told by a government employee living in Burgeo, "are allowed to run about like dirty little animals. It ought to be stopped. They ought to be sent away somewhere where they can get some discipline put into them!" The speaker's own young son, who had briefly blossomed in the Burgeo children's family, was himself about to be sent to England there to endure as best he might a rectification process which would turn him into a "proper" kind of man to fit the Brave New World.

The Burgeo children will miss him, for they had made him one of theirs. But they will all too soon face their own ordeal. As they reach adolescence their world is shattered brutally and abruptly. Suddenly they must enter into, and learn to suffer from, the general disintegration of the fabric of human life in the coves by the sounding sea. They must endure the death of certainty and the collapse of their sure shield.

It is an unparallelled pleasure to live amongst the children of the outports; they are soft-spoken, calm, imbued with an innate and entirely natural politeness, and generously uninhibited in the giving of their affections. It is unremittent agony to contemplate what lies ahead for their generation.

In the smaller outports of the Sou'west Coast, they can hope to find no remaining means of making a decent livelihood. In Burgeo, and other "growth-centres" of the planners, a few will find employment at the fish plant. Girls of fifteen or sixteen years of age will learn to stand for hours in a chilly and stinking shed, their hands reddening and roughening as they mechanically cull and pack the cold fish fillets that the production line inexorably spews at them. They do not endure this serfdom because they wish it, but because even the few dollars which they are paid may be vital to the survival of their parental homes. There is no real escape for them except into marriage or through emigration; and marriage in the New World they have been given brings an interminable and usually hopeless conflict against insurmountable economic odds.

Boys reaching young manhood may, if they are lucky enough to find a job at all, begin a meaningless pattern that can stretch out through all the years of their lives – they stand at the production tables filleting the fish that flow toward them – with no real hope ever of making enough money to realize the new way of life which they have been told, and must believe, is the only proper way. With marriage most of them will sink into a morass of debt as they attempt to acquire the shiny paraphernalia of the Admass society. They will exchange the outport home of their fathers for a facsimile of a mainland bungalow originally designed to stand in endless rows in some suburban development. They will attempt to fill these shoddy houses with cheap furniture that, in all too short a time, will degenerate with the house itself to become part of a new type of slum – the growth-centre slum, which is being created by the centralization planners.

A fearsome change comes over these young people when the shield goes down. They are bewildered and unbelieving to find the world of certainty is gone. Because they were happy children once, it takes them a long time to comprehend the depth of the betrayal. Because they spent their early years in a world of warm affection and never learned to hate, most of them will accept the unacceptable in silence; they will endure because they have not the capacity to turn against the leaders who have misled them.

This is the shape of things to come for those few who can manage to remain in the outports where they were born. But the majority cannot hope to cling to any kind of existence among the ruins of their own world. For these the future holds the blackest hours. They are the exiles, and they are the many. They are the people who are represented in that bitter jest: "Newfoundland's biggest export isn't fish no more, 'tis people." The moment inevitably will come to most of the children of the Sou'west Coast when they must board the coastal steamers, carrying their pathetic cardboard suitcases, and disappear into the maelstrom of a life they never knew, a life they have no training for and never wanted.

For as long as I live I shall remember an evening when I sat on a high rock overlooking the sea, and listened to the words of a young girl speaking about herself and her life.

"The worstest thing I know is that we got to go away. I watches the gulls following the boats out there and I wishes I was a gull sometimes, because nobody makes them go away from where they belongs. Those gulls are some lucky! They can stay and live in Burgeo until they dies. It won't be very long before they's nobody here except the gulls at all."

IT WON'T BE VERY LONG
BEFORE THERE'S
NOBODY HERE
EXCEPT THE GULLS
AT ALL